The Devil's in the Details
As told to Mark Bradford

I0607716

MARK BRADFORD

Printed in the United States of America
First Printing, 2023

Alchemy

ISBN-13: 978-1-7336622-7-7

markbradford.org

v1

DEDICATION

To the seekers of knowledge and enlightenment. To the readers and the dreamers. To the rare few who take and embrace the nuance instead of passing it by.

And to people who are nice to strangers.

ACKNOWLEDGEMENTS

To those who continue with me on this journey—old and new.
To those that take more drama than they give.
To those who have made me suffer less, not more.
To those that see my dream as clearly as I do.

Thank you.

The Devil's in the Details

The greatest trick wasn't convincing you that he doesn't exist...

As told to Mark Bradford.

The Devil's in the Details

PROLOGUE

This story was told to me as a narration, and I am in turn relating it to you as a narration. To avoid confusion, the chapters in which I am narrating to you are titled with the time it was in the cafe, everything else is the narration of my unusual guest, Simon.

I am not one to write the works of others, but since this literally and figuratively fell into my lap I was compelled to share.

CAFE - SUNDAY 8:05 AM

I met Simon—not surprisingly—at a cafe. As I try to get out at an early hour and write, it seemed that our schedules matched—at least on Sundays.

He was an older gentleman and dressed nicely including the cap that he wore. His all-white beard and hair were becoming of an elderly gentleman. I expected him to have a cane as it just seemed like it fit his general look, but he didn't. He always carried with him a stack of folders, a notebook, and old-looking papers. He never had a laptop and I never saw a phone. He'd usually come in, sit by himself and sip his drink. Staring out the window with an occasional glance to me was the norm.

Quick chats and tippings of his hat to me as he passed by to his chosen seat soon turned into him walking over and then sitting down. As his visits were inevitable and enjoyable, I adjusted my schedule so that I'd allow enough time for a chat with Simon.

Our chats were mostly surface things about the weather, the coffee, the younger generation, and me. He was definitely interested in all the random, seemingly-disjointed things I had my hands in. It especially piqued his interest that I wrote, but he wasn't interested in anything I'd *already* published for some reason. But one day that all changed.

He decided to tell me his story.

At first I thought it was a rather long joke, and hoped the punch line was worth it. And if it wasn't it was still nice to listen. But he kept going and wove a tale that pulled me in. I quickly forgot about what was on my laptop and ended up closing it as it felt almost rude to keep it open.

His story began with him being introduced to his professor when he was very young. Here is what he told me that Sunday in a quaint cafe with mediocre coffee.

OXFORD, 1966

I met my professor that crisp fall day. I was introduced to him by my friend Patrick. You see, at the time I was just a junior-year student in search of being an assistant. You call them teacher's assistants now— that's the jargon. But I wanted the experience and truth be told I wanted the inside track. Being an assistant meant bigger opportunities.

The man I was introduced to was well-known in college. He was gruff and self-absorbed and like most professors back then he seemed forever old. I disliked him the moment I met him, but my friend insisted with a twinkle in his eye. I had a quality that this man valued more than anything else—I would soon learn. My professor was a philosophy studies scholar with some experience in archeology. There were rumors about him and, well, he lived up to every one.

I came to see him in his office after that meeting for our official interview. His method was very formal—even for back then. We talked and he asked several of what I thought were prepared questions. His office was huge and as you can imagine stacks of papers and books littered the immediate area. He did not clean off his desk for the meeting and I was forced to dodge around the stacks to maintain eye contact as he moved around in his creaky chair.

"Well young man, you are interested in this position. I have looked at your paperwork and although it is acceptable I see nothing that stands out, so let me ask you some questions."

I sat up and did the best I could to answer him as he took off his spectacles.

"Yes sir."

He leaned forward, "Do you believe in God?"

I swallowed hard. This was not really something we talked about, and unlike now being an atheist wasn't all the rage. It was a personal thing.

"Professor?"

He did not like my lack of answer.

"It's a simple question, young man. *Do you believe in God?* Or is what a little bird whispered in my ear untrue?"

Before I could answer he slapped one of the piles.

"…and I am wasting my time again."

I struggled to answer him.

"I.. Well… What does… Well *no*."

He smiled a satisfied smile and leaned back a little.

"Good. Good. This is a good start. Honesty. Finally."

He put his spectacles back on and opened up his calendar book to jot a note. He shoved a piece of paper across his desk and pointed at a line with his fountain pen. A rather large blot accumulated as he waited for me to take the pen. "Sign here."
I admit I didn't read the document but it was a promise to not disclose

anything we worked on.   I believe they are called 'non-disclosure agreements.' I signed it.

"Tomorrow, first thing, this office. We will start. And here…"

He handed me a small binder of books. In those days it was just a leather wrap to keep books and papers together.

"Read through these. I will want to know your opinion."

I was taken aback and a bit lost and feeling in over my head. The big desk, the wall of books behind him, his brusqueness—it all moved so fast. I tried to squeak out a response.

"But professor. By tomorrow? You want…"

"Yes. First thing. Do not be late. And mind that you signed this."

He held up the NDA and then stood up.   I was excused. I left the office and didn't look back. I cursed my friend for what he'd gotten me into, but at the same time felt inflated importance because of what I was carrying under my arm. I admit I spent a good deal of time under a tree in the sun going over what he'd given me. They were personal notes, articles, and various scribblings. I was a bit surprised to see that he'd entrusted these to me. Though they were apparently only a tiny portion of his work, they were his personal notes. Unlike today they were all originals. If I lost them or spilled something on them it would be my undoing. I was excited and terrified, lest one even blow away in the wind. My neck hurt from looking over my shoulder in the beginning but soon I was lost in them.

The next day I was at his office bright and early. I waited outside his locked door for him to open it. He instead appeared in the hall next to me to unlock it and shoved some papers into my arms while he fumbled with keys. He began questioning me immediately as he grabbed the papers back and made his way to his desk.

"Well? What did you find?"

Find? I was confused. I wasn't really *looking* for anything. I was just absorbing as much as I could. I tried to memorize much of it in case there was a quiz.

He grabbed a book off of his shelf while simultaneously shelving two others. Then he sat down.

"Well Mr. Michaels, what did you find?"

Again he took off his glasses.

I could only blurt out what I thought he wanted me to say.

"I think your work is very thorough and I think we are a good fit for research. I'd be honored to study under you and I promise my beliefs will not get in the way."

I had practiced that response all morning and thought I could work it into whatever he asked me, which I assume was about our compatibility. I was dead wrong.

"No no no!"

He slammed his fist on the desk. He wasn't a violent man, and the fist was very weak indeed and just done for effect I think. I think I literally bit my tongue at that point lest I say anything else to upset him. But boy was I confused. He explained at last.

"Mr. Michaels I did not give you those notes so you could cozy up to me. I gave you those notes to see what they would spark within you."

The look on his face told me he was more interested in what would come out of my mouth next than anything else so far. I took a blind leap of faith—no pun intended.

"Well, I just don't get it. It's just obvious that the people in your notes are just adjusting their experiences to match what they want to believe."

He stared and said just two words: "Go on."

"They are good notes. You are meticulous and I found them easy to read. I think that you are…"
I froze. It was going so well. He leaned forward which was my signal to

10

get some confidence.

"…biased."

He paused and waved his hand lackadaisically. I took that to mean I should expand.

"Well sir, professor, I mean, your conclusions are all based on there being an outside force. You think it is all happening for a reason. And I think you seem to think, well, that these incidents are all tied together."

"And you don't?"

"Well no, sir, I don't. None of them are tied together. At best they are coincidences. You only gave me—those were only some of your notes right?"

"Yes, a portion, son."

"Yes well, I can only tell so much in an evening—from a portion."

I realized I was doing pretty well, and had absorbed a lot. But really it was just a sample. Oddly he didn't object to my disagreement.

"So you'd chalk it all up to coincidence? To people wanting to believe what they want to believe—I suppose you'd say."

I smiled a tiny bit.

"Well yes, that is the easier, more logical way."

"And I cannot convince you otherwise."

It was not a question so I felt safe in being honest.

"No. You cannot."

When he abruptly reached over the desk I almost fell over, but then I realized he was shaking hands with me. He looked almost ecstatic but then his face became serious as I vigorously shook his hand and stood up.

"Mr. Michaels you will promise me to always apply this 'logic' to what we work on, and to never ever hold back. If I think you are being dishonest with me I will let you go on the spot, and you will have to travel far and away to further your education."

It was a threat and a promise, and my heart sank temporarily. But then I realized that having the freedom to actually be honest was a very good stipulation. I mean, that's what caused me to be an Atheist in the first place.

After that, I worked very closely with him. My friend Patrick who had initially recommended me (and I assume was the little bird in his ear) seemed very pleased with his connection. Others in the college were quite judgmental to me about my work with him. As you can imagine religious studies on that level were quite polarizing, even back then. Fortunately, none of them knew about my actual beliefs—they just assumed mine were in line with the professor's.

And so it was that I worked closely with him. It was more of a job for credits and clout than anything else, and there were those that were confused by my assistance with a professor that did not teach anything I was pursuing. At the time I was involved in other studies. I won't bore you with them because as you see they were quickly forgotten.

The notes I was given were a bunch of case studies that he had pursued with people who had experiences. These experiences were... negative.

I thought it was very possible that he was just trying to convince me to believe in God and that my friend had set me up. But the more I read the less these sounded like the kinds of happenings that one would use to convince someone. It was quite the opposite. So why try to convince me of something I already believe?

But when I read some of his notes I came to understand that he was attempting to demonstrate that a higher power *was* involved.

I just wasn't sure which one.

—

In the coming weeks, we went over more case studies and he always seemed to appreciate my take on them. I felt absolutely free to state my honest assessment of them.   Most times they were counter to his findings.   He would make notes and literally draw connections on the papers from one incident to another.   His notes were quite eccentric I suppose, but also very scientific in a mad scientist sort of way.

These days you people are all about conspiracy theories and they're all over the internet.   So what he was proposing I suppose would make a popular Youtube page.

SIMON'S MUM

Growing up where I did afforded me some luxuries. I was close to both of my parents but lost my father at an early age. As an only child, my mum became my best friend growing up and it impacted my life. I knew it was bittersweet for me to go off to college, and I was lucky for her to fund it.

We stayed close and there were so many moments that I will cherish for a very long time.

She taught me so much growing up, and I can still smell the pies she baked—nothing like what you have today. They were simpler and subtle. Everything is so intense now.

She was always so energetic—so full of life—even after my dad passed. I knew she would never remarry as they were both very much in love. It was an example I strived to live by.

Her care packages to the college were things of beauty and always made for an event when they arrived. Patrick and I would make a night of it, opening the box and making an inventory of all the goods inside. Once I told her this she started sending even more because she said my 'friend Patrick can't just watch you have all the fun.' It was a grand time at college pursuing my studies, the newfound work I had with my professor, and attempting to explore the world and all it had to offer.

"Simon. My love. My dear lad."

My mother was always so formal.

Many a day was spent talking about going off to college and the wonders of the world that I would learn. I never told my mum about my beliefs but I think she suspected. She wasn't a very devout woman, but she had a great deal of faith and it manifested itself in some of the comments she would make.

I think it was what I didn't say that spoke more about my choices than what I did.

She never asked and just set a very good example for me. Like my dad, she was someone I looked up to. And maybe unlike most college boys, I missed her a bit more than they did.

Mark Bradford

THE HALLWAY

I typically didn't see the professor interact with the other staff. I knew how stern he was with students, and—truth be told—philosophy is not something you can just check the answer book on. There's a bit of interpretation. But, I felt that he was fair and knew his stuff.

There were the usual rumblings from students on his methods and how dry his teachings were. I have to say that my work with him never really entered into his lectures, and after getting to know him for a bit I only imagine just how much effort it took for him to be proper. Trust me, the other teachers never let a little professionalism stand in the way of some good, hearty personal bias.

But one day I got to see firsthand what was going on behind the scenes. He was speaking in the hall with two other professors.

The professors looked upset as he addressed one of them.

"Denis, my thought on the matter is that I'd strongly prefer to not hear yours."

"Why Malcolm, I do believe you are upset with me."

"Upset?" The professor shifted the multitude of books in his hands in an attempt to find his keys.

"Yes Malcolm. Upset. I was merely voicing my opinion on the matter. I presume you appreciate spirited conversation. It is, after all, what you are known for."

Professor Gabriel froze, turned his head, and looked down and over his glasses at his antagonist.

"And now I know you are joking, Archie."

He paused, took a deep breath, and then summarily ignored him as he introduced his key to the lock. As the door creaked open the silence was deafening.

I would stand in the hallway for some minutes afterward to ensure that he hadn't known I watched the whole thing. Eventually, I entered his office with a quiet knock at the open door.

"Did you enjoy the show, Mr. Michaels?"

He said this without even looking up as I entered the office. It was at times like this that I was convinced he was clairvoyant.

I eventually got through the awkward conversation by remembering that the professor valued honesty above all. He was more than willing to divulge what that was all about.

"I know this is difficult to believe, but there are some here that are not particularly fond of my methods. I have no doubt that they are rather taken with me as a human of course, and it is merely my methods they take exception with."

"What is their... what, why do they..."

He finished re-shelving some of his books and moving paperwork about his desk. I was sure that it was future work for me. My question was less than eloquent and I stumbled over it. I would never really feel comfortable around the man—always intimidating was he.

"The staff at large feel that I'm distracted. I imagine that—distracted, me?"

"Distracted by what sir?"

I knew the answer. He knew the answer.

"Well, I suppose my project. Our project, Mr. Michaels."

It was the first time I felt we were working together on something. Up til now I felt like I was doing the best I could for him as a hired hand but felt no ownership. But his use of 'our' stirred up feelings I didn't know I had regarding this work.

"Sir, I don't see that you are distracted. I haven't seen…"

He waved me off politely—clearly seeing that I was trying to be supportive.

"Well, perhaps you have become biased in your perceptions of me."

"No sir I don't think I have."

I smiled a weak smile. I think I was actually a little concerned. You see, professors are always intimidating—at least they *were*. They were always the Alpha and Omega when it came to university, and they all seemed to be self-contained. The thought of him not being the apex meant in a strange way that I wasn't as comfortable or protected.

"Well, I can allow a little bias towards me, as long as it doesn't seep into your work with me."

"No of course…"

I think in his own way he was expressing affection and allowing me to do the same. He just labeled it as bias.

He went on to tell me that there had been questions and now there was to be an inquiry into his teaching practice. It was all so secretive, and a behind-closed-doors kind of affair. Academic staff never showed chinks in their armor so it was surprising that they would have a conversation outside his door. And I was just as surprised that he would even discuss it with me.

"Well, what is to happen now?"

It was an awkward way to ask.

"Oh, I suppose there will be some sort of meeting in which the others will point their fingers at me, cite my work, perhaps even collect testimony from students—no doubt the ones in particular that I intended to fail."

He didn't look alarmed at this at all. To me, this sounded like the worst thing that could happen to him and he was completely unfazed.

"Well, sir if there's anything I can do."

At this, he looked intrigued.

"Do? What would you *do* Mr. Michaels? Please elaborate."

He actually smiled. I took a deep breath and collected my thoughts.

"Well I mean I would appear for you and…"

"Go on…"

"And say a few words, or testify to your…"

"To my what?"

He was not making this easy.

"Professor, I would just be…"

He stared at me intently. It was rather accusatory. He looked at me like I was the one under scrutiny. I felt like it was I that was on trial and not him. I know I stared at him for only a second but it felt like minutes as I finished the sentence.

"…honest."

At this, I saw him change. His face softened and I think I saw the real professor in that moment—a man who was driven, committed, and full of conviction but ultimately alone and vulnerable. I knew then I was the only advocate he had.

"Of course, you would, Simon."

They were the gentlest, kindest words he ever said to me. After that, he went back to focusing on his work, being gruff and then asking why I had come to visit him. It was of course to bring more notes to him about his work.

I felt the subject closed and didn't want to risk reopening the subject but felt compelled to ask. So after what was easily an hour I finally did.

"Sir, when is the inquiry if I may ask?"

"Oh not as soon as they'd like."

"Why is that?"

"Because their proposed date does not fit in my schedule."

"Your schedule?"

"Yes, they are going to have to wait and they don't like that."

Wait for what I thought but didn't voice it. He heard it nonetheless, apparently.

"They will have to wait until we return."

He seemed almost playful at this and was goading me into prompting him, but I was just too confused.

"Ah… We?"

"They will have to wait until we return from Cairo."

PATRICK

I had been so immersed in helping the professor that I hardly had much time to do anything else. My other studies were suffering a bit but fortunately, I just saw sleep as an option. I'm sure most college kids are that way even today.

But my friend Patrick became concerned and he all but shanghaied me into having a pint with him.

The place was off campus a bit and not frequented by the students much. It had a reputation for being stuffy and thus was Patrick's secret. I didn't drink much so it wasn't something I was aware of.

The tables, benches, and bar were so rich and vivid with polished wood. It was beautiful and we were definitely the youngest in the pub, so we kept to our manners and didn't smile too much, but Patrick couldn't hold in his excitement.

"Simon man! You made it!"
I flinched as he rustled my hair and grabbed me around the neck. I let

him have his fun and melted into the booth. I couldn't help but feel better just from the small amount of physical contact. He was my friend and I'd all but ignored him.

"It's your fault, Pat." I smiled. "You got me the in with the Prof."

He pointed at me with a proud look.

"I did! That I did. I'm glad you were able to escape his clutches though."

My eyes were wide and I shook my head. Then I signed.

"You're telling me, man. It's been…"

"What!? Spill it. I want to know what I got you into!" He sipped his beer and found it obviously to his liking. I sipped mine too and had almost forgotten the taste of it.

"Ahh Pat. This was a good idea. It's so intense, you feel me? So much research. So many notes. He's meticulous. But it's all the same."

"What is?"

"The notes. The articles. It's, well, it's different, I mean different people and all…"

Pat held his glass—not sure whether to put it down and talk or sip it again and listen. I kept rambling.

"I do my best. And he thinks I'm doing well. I review the notes, I look them over, I meet with him, and then disagree. I'm…"

"What? Well what…?"

"I'm checking his work. I don't really come to any conclusions. I just keep telling him it's all unrelated."

"What's unrelated."

I put my glass down—it was almost empty already. I had to take a deep breath. Since I'd never talked about it outside of meetings with the professor I hadn't really summarized it yet.
"This is going to sound crazy. The professor has some sort of theory.

26

It's…"

I scrunched my face up.

"It's…they…"

"Are you takin' the piss?"

Patrick laughed and was genuinely enjoying my difficulty in explaining.

"I think he thinks the devil's afoot."

His face dropped.

"Are you serious? You checking his work and he's trying to prove that the devil's afoot? How so? He's muckin' about and my friend Simon is here to prove it's so?"

"Yes."

"Well, how's he gonna do that? And how you gonna prove him wrong— or right?"

"Well, I…"

"Oh this is good. This is *so* good."

Patrick was delighted. To me, it was a bit more serious.

"Patrick. Don't know when it's going to end? Maybe he'll just give up or be sick of me. But here's the thing—the more honest I am the more he likes it."

"And you keep telling him there's nothin' there?"

"Yes. There's no connection."

"Well then maybe he's just wrong. He'll figure it out, write you a glowing letter of recommendation you can use to further your degree or get whatever job you want. You know, I don't even know what you're pursuing."

That's when I looked sheepish.

"What? What'd I say, Simon?"

"Patrick. I have let things slip. I mean, I'm pretty much ignoring my classes and grades, I'm in so deep. It's exhausting, reading about this, learning, etc."

"I'm sorry... hell I hope not too much...?"

I just stared.

"Simmy you muppet."

He looked genuinely upset, but even more so something else that didn't really suit him—he looked parentally disappointed.

I stared and felt empty as he continued to stare. It was my turn to talk and he was just going to keep waiting. I can still feel the discomfort.

"OK, ok. I think I am going to fail. There's no way I can keep my grades up. I've let go of everything and I think..."

"You think what."

"I don't know. I still want to be an architect."

"Well of course you do! Simmy this was supposed to be a side job for you. This is just a feather in the cap at the expense of the old codger. You help him out and read his musty notes and he gives you a letter. You make a whole lotta bread and I stay at your mansion in the States."

He blinked as if resetting to the previous conversation.

"Patrick, why did you recommend me?"

"I'm sorry. Well, what exactly are these notes about?"

Patrick sounded angry—not at me, but on my behalf. He didn't like that things were slipping.

"Simon I recommended you because I thought you would be exceptional at it and that..."

"...and that I don't believe?"

"No, *that you would benefit from it.*"

"But you told him."

"He asked."

Now it was Pat's turn to look sheepish.

"Yeah, I did. But he asked. I know it's personal and private, but the way he asked was so... odd. Like he was desperately needing it to be true."

"Sounds like what we are doing now."

"Is he...obsessive?"

I nodded. I hadn't given that much thought. Meeting with Pat was like living in the pond and then coming up for air. I finally had time to think.

"Yes. Come to think of it Pat, *yes*. He is very obsessive. And it scares me. I think I've just been riding it out. And maybe just counting the days."

Patrick squinted at me.

"There's something else, isn't there."

I looked down at the table, then at him. But before I could talk he blurted something out, and he was staring at me.

"You believe it! You're starting to believe it?! What?"

He slapped the table, causing a number of the regulars to look over at us. Some of the looks were not kind. We were on thin ice. I tried to calm him down.

"Patrick. Easy... I've read so much, maybe I am seeing a pattern, or maybe I'm going cross-eyed. Or I'm just giving up."

"Naw. That's not you Simmy. You don't give up. You'll put the old bastard in his grave before you sell out. There must be something there for you to feel that way—I see it in your eyes."

I shook my head in disbelief at my own feelings. I was feeling exposed, and a little crazy I suppose.

"Well, there is sort of pattern. Once you see it you can't stop seeing it. No, I don't believe in any of that nonsense, but there is a lot of this."

He held onto his empty glass with both hands and looked down at it. It was like I had a redheaded potter sitting across from me. Slowly he looked up. I could see some regret on his face.

"A lot of what, friend?"

I looked over to the crowd and then back at him.

"Suffering."

"Suffering? You looking at hospital paperwork? We all suffer."

"It's more than that. It's...a pattern. It's inevitable."

He laughed. "What, no happy endings?"

"No."

"No?"

His face was changing to reflect the somber responses.

"Well, not really."

"Simon man, that's depressing."

"There's more."

"Oh?" He raised an eyebrow. To me his eyebrows always looked like odd orange caterpillars. And now one was arching his back.

"The articles are just the evidence."

"Evidence of what."

"Oh boy, I'm gonna need another drink."

The conversation was like going to a priest for confession and not receiving a penance. I think the meeting made me truly realize that I had destroyed my dreams of being an architect.

And instead was chasing a fantasy with an obsessive old man.

CAFE - 9:40 AM

"Hidden message?"

My cafe guest seemed jarred by my question. As Simon spoke I was silent, but he'd dropped it as a punch line so I had to ask. I didn't know if he was going to continue.

He smiled a frustrated smile—the kind one uses just before telling you to invest in gold from a certain company.

"Yes Mark. A message. That's… Oh, I'm boring you already."

"No no!"

I tried to calm him and immediately felt bad for apparently interrupting. He continued.

"Yes, that's what it was all about. A message. The professor was looking for a message and…"

"What message?"

I all but slapped my hand to my mouth. I did it again.

"Well Mark…"

He raised his coffee to his lips, sipped it, and then didn't look back at me as he finished.

"The message from the Devil himself."

THE MESSAGE ON THE PLANE, 1967

A year into helping the professor we went on our first journey together. As I said he seemed to have an interest in archeology but did not possess a degree in it. I learned that the faculty kept their distance and most had a healthy amount of respect for the man. The man was meticulous at keeping notes, remembering facts, and always speaking his mind. But he was never threatening and always respected the boundaries of his fellows in academia. They were free to conduct themselves however they liked without any judgment from him, so they in turn paid little mind to what seemed like a string of pet projects. In addition, the professor always taught what was expected, so none of the things we discussed ever made it into a lesson plan or a curriculum. He flew under the radar as you would say, and it was our secret. At least this was my solid perception of things and I had no reason to question it, and the altercation in the hallway seemed to be all but forgotten.

He had a way of just making things go away through sheer stamina.

Our first visit was to the middle east. I had never been there and the professor kindly funded the travel. Having a passport, traveling by plane and the prospect of new cultures had me enamored. These were exceptional things at the time! Now people will visit other countries and ancient cultures just as tourists on a whim. Everything is electronically scheduled. Not so back then. You had better have your paperwork or travel with a dignitary.

My professor wasn't a dignitary, but as an Oxford professor of tenure he had the clout to protect us should things go awry. And anything we did could just be part of our academic endeavors.

People nowadays are enamored of ancient cultures and believe all sorts of things about them. Back then it was more about discovering writings, languages, and the people that created them. The professor was interested in languages like Coptic Egyptian, Sumerian, and Sanskrit. We believed these were the oldest languages and whatever he was looking for would be found there.

The professor seemed to take a tiny bit of joy at both my discomfort and excitement at international travel. Though I'd been on a plane before, this was a trip of monumental proportions. I was animated and nervous and for once I was not a very passive audience. He was as trapped with me as I was with him. I studied as many of the examples of writing as I could, though I was not as natural with language as was he. And truth be told the bumpy ride made it all little difficult to concentrate without getting sick, but I did my best to make out the little triangles on the paper in front of me.

"Professor, what do you hope to find?"

"Find?"

"Well yes, what do you hope to find there? You said there were no meetings, but instead just a travel guide from the office of antiquities. Is it more case studies about people?"

"Why, the message of course. I want to see how far back it goes."

"The message? How far back?"

"Yes, son. We are going to prove that it's there. If I'm right it goes as far back as there is language."

I thought about this for a while. My stomach felt sick. You see, up until now there were vague things afoot. We were collecting data and I had the freedom to be honest. But now he named the thing we were looking for: a message. It was then I believed he was crazy, and I was trapped in a tin can high above the North Atlantic Ocean. As you say now I was reconsidering my 'life choices.'

"Oh don't look so scared Mr. Michaels."

"I'm...not. I'm just a little air sick."

He pointed to the bag in front of me.

"No no sir, I'll be fine."

We sat in silence for at least another hour as I switched from staring ahead at the bag and looking out the window. All this work was essentially harmless. I was acting as a social worker in a way— gathering information about people's lives and such. But we didn't interact with them. My job was essentially to just confirm or dispute what the professor proposed. It had no beginning and was just an endless stream of case studies.

But now we were talking about something spooky. This brought it to a whole new level. I looked back out the window.

The clouds were pretty and calming. The calmness began to overtake the sense of dread and panic. The more I stared, the less I thought, the better I felt. My mum was far away and I missed her now more than ever. I would seek her out upon my return. She was quite pleased with my travel with a professor. Her latest care package seemed to be twice the size it normally was, much to Patrick's delight.

"You think I am crazy."

The professor was looking down his nose, through his glasses at a piece of paper. I whipped my head around from the window to him and he showed no signs of speaking. I wasn't sure if I'd heard it or perhaps if he had been speaking to someone else. But then he spoke again without looking, matter-of-factly.

"You do, don't you?"

"Yes."

I blurted it out. I immediately closed my eyes and would have literally slapped my forehead had I not been so taken off guard.

He grabbed a pen, laid the paper down, and circled something on it. Again without looking he spoke.

"Do you recall why I chose you?"

I cleared my throat and waved away some of the cigarette some that decided to invade the space between us just then.

"Because... you valued my honesty? In fact, you threatened to expel me if I was ever dishonest."

"Yes."

He spoke earnestly and without malice.

"So if you are being honest—even if you think I am indeed crazy—then you have not broken the terms of our agreement, and are still providing value."

I was relieved. He was far more predictable than I understood at the time. I took a deep breath as he shoved the paper over to my lap.

It was the little triangles I mentioned—cuneiform. He had circled a few of them and written 'tiny parts/pieces?' next to it.

You're going to help me check my work. I could be wrong about this. If I am will you tell me?

I glanced up at his face and then back to the paper.

"Of course."

"I'm glad you're still with us, Mr. Michaels."

Mark Bradford

TO SEEK IS TO FIND - CAIRO

We had been traipsing around Egypt for well over a week.   It was hot, and I was reminded of the crash just a year prior.   Though it was big news I had somehow forgotten on the flight there.   Maybe it was my mind protecting me, or maybe ultimately my fear of the professor was stronger than worrying about air travel.

Regardless I felt like all we did was walk around. We had very little exposure to anything I would consider to be antiquities. We never met with anyone of note and were not given access to anything that would have something ancient recorded on it.

It was at this time that my doubts were starting to outweigh my faith in the man.

You see, even though I thought what he was doing was nonsense, I knew that he was applying a very strict code of learning and method to his— what do you say now? Oh, he had a method to his madness.   But now I was thousands of miles from home and the quest he thought we were on was just.

The day before we were to leave I became very ill. Looking back I am sure it was all of the exotic foods I sampled. Give me some Dippy eggs and soldiers or a proper Shepherd's pie, not the questionable exotic delights of that faraway land. Oh, I know you can get anything in America now and nothing is sacred, but I wanted my comfort food, and I wanted my mum to make it.

I couldn't have either. I was miserable and that day after throwing up to the point of dry heaves the professor left me to my own devices. He said I just needed some water and something salty.

I barely had any strength left but somehow found the means to yell at him.

"You don't care! You dragged me all the way here for your…"

I held my stomach. It churned. I squeaked out the last word.

"…fantasy."

The look on his face was horrific. It was the first time I'd spoken up to him. I think he was most taken aback by the fact I didn't address him as 'sir.'

He just stared. For a second I thought I saw sadness.

He stopped at the door.

"Mister… Simon. You will be all right. You should really expand your palate."

He grabbed his hat and opened the door but didn't leave before leaving me with some perplexing words.

"I've made some arrangements for you. They should suit your… needs while I am away. I shall return tomorrow I think."

The messed up face I made at his back as he left was not lost on him, especially since he abruptly turned around to add five words.
"And don't leave without me."

I sat in the hot room with all the drapes closed. I disliked the man very much. I was lost. I thought of all I had given up to be his attendant. It never included teaching but instead focused on this unending search for something invisible. I was just his slave meticulously checking his work with no end in sight. There was no happy ending. Either he gave up and all the work was for naught or worse, we'd somehow find the devil.

To my surprise, he had arranged for some food I was used to. I know he must have paid a pretty penny for it too. It was—as I had complained to him many times—proper British food. I slowly nursed myself to health with that and a lot of water.

He did of course come back and was cheered visibly. To my disappointment, I learned it was due to his findings, and not seeing me a as hue other than green.

"I found something."

Frankly, I didn't want to hear it. I just wanted to go home, and formally break off my engagement with the good professor.

But unfortunately I listened.

I don't know if I was just happy to be eating real food and feeling in good health, or if the surroundings gave it all a shroud of mystery and importance, but his words had an impact on me.

We were at an outdoor market and all manner of people milled about along with animals of varying sizes. it was overwhelming having been cooped up in my room. Now the sunlight, the people, and the beasts assaulted all of my senses at once.

I reached for my tea and the professor moved my hand away lest I put it down onto the center of his attention: his notes.

He excitedly spoke while unrolling a scroll on top of things. He showed me pictures and hieroglyphics and even a photo of a wall. Apparently, we hadn't really come here to explore pyramids or detailed work on the history of the ancient Egyptians, but instead to verify some things—and to meet up with an associate of the professor.

It was this man that had provided some of the missing pieces.

The professor moved as a blur and spoke quickly.

"Do you see this, young Simon? These all say the same thing."

He was moving his index finger from photo to writing to his notes to an etching, and he didn't seem to care if he smeared any of it. I looked closely while holding onto my tea cup for dear life. I couldn't read any of it.

"I don't know what that says, sir."

He wasn't mad, but instead nodded as if I'd agreed with him.

"Yes, yes… It's all the same, and each language points to the other for confirmation you see."

He smiled. My mind raced.

"Confirmation of what sir?"

He grabbed a scroll that had snapped back into a roll and shoved it at me to get it out of his way.

"And this? And this. There isn't even a way to say this properly, but I know what they meant."

I stared at the side of his head while he looked intently at the tabletop's offerings. He immediately snapped his head to the left and stared right at me. The intense look drained from his face as he saw my confusion.

"Well why are you looking at me, boy, look at the…"

Stopping himself he took off his glasses and rubbed his eyes. When he put them back on he was a different man.

"Simon. All of these languages and civilizations are telling us the same thing. These parts all go together."
"But how could this go together with this?"

I pointed from the cuneiform to the hieroglyphics

"Exactly."

"Exactly *what* sir?"

I was cognizant of my recent outburst and wanted to give him as much attention as possible. As I said I was sort of trapped, after all. And I felt a little guilty.

"Well young man, if you and I wanted to write a letter together how would we do it?"

"Well, I suppose we'd get together and meet and.."

"What if we cannot meet?"

He pushed the cuneiform to one end of the table where he sat and some of the notes to the other where I sat.

"We are separated by great distance. No phones."

"Well..."

"And I die thousands of years before you even start your half of the letter."

"Ahh... um, I suppose."

"And I cannot read your handwriting."

"Professor! I don't know. It's impossible."

I was going to ask if he was joking when the waiter came and the professor suddenly had a grin. He picked up the notes he had on his side of the table and handed them to the waiter.

"Would you please hand this to the young man?"

The waiter looked confused and saw that the professor could have just handed it to me himself.

Except that he was dead.

I got it. We couldn't communicate directly but a third party could bridge the gap.

I accepted the gesture and put it down in front of me. The confused waiter walked away once we said we didn't need anything.

"But then, who is the waiter? He would have to outlive us both. And you said we were separated by..."

That's when I got a chill down my spine that had nothing to do with my recovery from food poisoning.

All the professor did was nod, and I've never seen him look happier.

—

On the plane ride back I asked the professor what the actual message was. What was so important that it not just be passed from language to language, but be hidden in such a way that only an eternal being could facilitate the message across civilizations.

"You are familiar with Baudelaire I assume?"

I nodded. Most knew of the prominent French poet, and I had actually quoted him one in an argument at university—in an attempt to sound smart in front of a girl. It worked.

"I've read his poetry sir."

"And his stories?"

"Yes."

I sounded less convincing since I was only aware of his poetry.

"'The greatest trick the Devil ever pulled was...'"
It was a test, at thousands of feet in the air. I needn't have worried as the

professor finished it immediately.

"'to convince man that he didn't exist.'"

I nodded, then looked confused. With the utmost confidence, and with conviction the professor added, "That's not the message."

"Oh!"

I waited. And waited. Finally, I spoke.

"Professor, what *is* the message then? What did you find?"

"Well, I don't think it's something you would believe son."

I took a deep breath. This was all so trying. I'd been so honest and forthcoming and now he seemed to be playing games.

"Professor, respectfully, I deserve to know."

"True. Well said..."

"And whether I believe it or not is up to me and..."

"Son."

"Yes sir?"

"You can stop now. You convinced me."

I stared. Even when I won I felt like I lost. He continued.

"What I have learned is that there is a message... and a warning."

"OK. And you learned both? What is the message? What is the warning?"

He looked tired.

"The message is that what we understand about reality is wrong. We have been misled, and the very act of trying to find this message will spell your doom."

I was oddly relieved, and I smiled. This took him aback. Once we got back I would stop all this nonsense. The old crazy man could continue his pursuit of the message that couldn't be described, and I would excuse myself. I'd put in my time and had proven that all we were doing was chasing our tails. Let the administration look into his pursuits—I'd be long gone by then anyway.

Mark Bradford

GRACE AND APLOMB

The first person I wanted to see upon my return was my mum, and I made a beeline for her to visit. The professor as well as others made demands on my time, and we were almost done with the break, but she was a sight for sore eyes. That is, she would have been, but as it turned out things had taken a turn for the worse.

She looked at me with kind eyes that held back the sadness. She knew what was happening—we all did. It was why someone from the hospital had taken residence with her that autumn. She had so little time left.

"Mum!"

I ran to her side. It was an adjustment to just sit bedside. She was the kind of woman that would run up and hug even strangers which was quite a sight back then.

Not today. And not ever again. I had tried hugging her while she lay still but I couldn't pull it off and I could tell it made her ache—not just from the pain of being touched, but the pain of not being touched.

"How are you doing at university? Are you keeping up your grades? Are you eating?"

Though she spoke slowly I knew not to interrupt as it was the same three questions lately. She was passively guiding our conversation you see. She knew the more she got me talking the less we would focus on her and the time left.

It dwindled.

I had already told her everything there was to tell about the trip on the tele, and she insisted on no souvenirs for obvious reasons. I was glad to return to what seemed so normal.

I did my best as always to keep talking, to keep smiling, and to fill the time and space with my love for her. I knew it was what she wanted although an onlooker would have thought me selfish. It was quite the opposite.

"I have to go, Simon."

Those were her last words to me. She made the effort to let go and she died that night in her sleep.

The doctor told me she wasn't in pain but I knew she just hid it well— with grace and with aplomb.

She had many days ahead of her, but I think with losing my dad and me going off to University she really had no reason to fight. I didn't begrudge her back then. It was her choice, but I wanted her to live forever.

CAFE: 1PM

"I'm sorry Simon, I understand it's hard sometimes."

My awkward sentence was meant to comfort him.

"Oh, it is. You have no idea, or do you?"

I smiled for some reason—perhaps it was the sudden attention and the intense way he was looking at me. Up until now, he was mostly a jovial storyteller, but now there was a new intensity to his eyes. I answered him nonchalantly.

"Well, I've had my own ups and downs. I think I have learned that everything is cyclical."

"Yes. How is your family?"

"My...? Oh, my kids?"

"No, siblings and so forth."

"Oh, I'm sure they are good."

"And your kids, you said you had two?"

"Yes, they are good. As far as I know."

"You got a lady?"

I took a breath and tried to respond with as much humor as I could muster as he glanced at the absence of a ring.

"Did we just enter the 20 questions lightning round or something? I mean is the story over?" I was hoping that was said with as much humor as planned but I think it was less than friendly and I regretted it.

I had no intention of going into detail about my family—extended or otherwise—and my love life. I shook my head and was a little irritated. He was a stranger that had just told a story for hours so far and then just stopped out of nowhere to interrogate me. I could feel the defensiveness reaction rising within and took another breath. My smile probably did not look genuine. It was not.

"Did I say something wrong?"

"It's just a little disorienting, Simon. You know?"

"I was just asking about your life."

I shook my head quickly and sort of shrugged.

"My life is fine. The usual. Not much different than other people."

"Exactly."

Now I was even more annoyed, as I had often complained that this was not the case, that I've had some crazy things happen and that sometimes I …

I realized I was upset at him for assuming the positive. Why was I so annoyed? I came clean.

"OK, Simon. I admit I am a little annoyed. I mean a life is a lot to describe to people. There are a lot of nuances. Things go wrong. Maybe other people go through the same, maybe they don't. Sorry."

He seemed unfazed but appreciated my apology. He was digging for something and I wanted to know what it was.

"Mark I wanted to prove a point to you."

"That being?"

"The very thing I learned on my journey."

"Oh." I thought I understood, but then I didn't, so I repeated myself.

"Oh? What is that? Wait! I think I know. I always say 'Suffering equals experience and experience equals wisdom!' Is that what you are trying to teach me?"

I went from being annoyed to being a bit self-absorbed in my brilliance. He was obviously telling me this very long story for a reason.

"That there isn't a message?" I was sure the story was over.

"I didn't say that."

CHRISTMAS, 1967

Oxford had three terms, and we had about three weeks for Christmas. Patrick asked me to come home with him and his family—to stay for the vacation. He knew I had nothing to go home to.

I agreed but I only spent a few days after Christmas with them. They were a nice enough family but the nicer they were the more I missed my mum... and my dad.

Funny that after my mum died I started to think of my father more. My brain sort of lined up their deaths in a way as if they both left at the same time instead of being separated by a decade or so.

Funny how that works. I don't know if my mind did that to just file things away easier, or if it was some sort of trick I played on myself to feel worse. For whatever reason it worked—I felt worse.

In fact, I felt so bad that I didn't want to be with a family that was lucky enough to have living, breathing parents.

Selfish of me, wasn't it?

Patrick did the best he could to tolerate me that Christmas. I think I brought the whole bunch down and they quickly learned there was nothing they could say to console me.

So it was for the better that I left, and indeed I did.

Since my mum's place was sold I took some of the money in the bank and did a bit of travel.

It was the best decision I could have made as it was a rather pleasant and expensive distraction.

I tried to keep my mind clear of all this nonsense. This was my last chance to focus on my schoolwork when I came back and graduate properly. I needed to make Mum and Dad proud.

Of course, I thought this while I was frivolously spending their money.

Mark Bradford

THOUGHTS AND...

"Mr. Michaels—Simon, may I ask you a question."

We had been back to work for only a short while and I admit it was hard to get back in the grind, as it were. I was still formulating a way to part ways with him. I think I was half in and half out.

The professor's timidness took me by surprise. And he had used my first name. I think this might have been the first time.

"Uh, yes sir."

"Well first of all again I want to offer my condolences on the passing of your mother."

"Well thank you, sir. I appreciate the kindness."

He was tiptoeing around something.

"What do you do at the time of her passing?"

"Excuse me, sir?"
He searched for words—an odd action from someone who seemed like he always had a prepared speech.

"At the funeral, at her passing. I know you are in mourning, son."

"Yessir, I am."

"So what do you think… about? Where do your thoughts go?"

It took me a while to understand what he was asking.

"Do you mean do I pray sir?"

"Yes."

He seemed genuinely curious, like looking at a new animal in captivity.

"Uh, no. No, I don't. I wouldn't do that. What would I do that?"

"Oh. OK. Thank you, son. Thank you for indulging me. I meant no disrespect to your parent."

"None taken."

It was awkward and made me feel a little uneasy. He was a scientist and asked a lot of questions, I suppose.

Just when I thought he was going to shamble away he asked another question and startled me.

"What's your motivation here."

I froze. I felt like he was accusing me. Or perhaps he was on to me. Could he tell that my heart was no longer in it?

"What? My motivation? Here? With you? With helping you I mean?"

"Yes.

I thought about this for an embarrassingly long time, I must admit.

"Well sir, I suppose it has evolved a bit."

"Go on…"

I scratched my head and continued.

"When my friend, Patrick, suggested I talk to you I wanted to have the extra credits and experience."

"Yes?"

"But then I met you and I was… terrified that I'd made the wrong decision because…"

"I made you sign a document?"

"No… No sir."

He waited.

"Because it seemed that my belief was somehow important."

"It was. And it still is."

"But I don't really have a belief, sir."

"You do. Do you not think that a lack of belief is just as important as having one?"

"Well, I…"

It was a genuine question from him so he waited for an answer.

"Well, I never thought of it that way… But sir, I think that it is, er, was a personal thing, and accepting me based on that wasn't something I expected or was really comfortable with."

"Then why did you sign up with me?"

"Well, I really needed the extra credits and my mum always told me to pursue the extra circulars, and ingratiate myself with the professors."

"Your mother was a smart woman."

"Thank you, sir."

"But that's not really why I chose you."

"You didn't? I mean, it wasn't?"

"No, it was an indicator of how your mind worked. That's not to say all people who believe as you do think the same way, or vice versa. But I know that you are an honest person. And what I needed more than anything was honesty in an assistant."

"Thank you, professor. I appreciate that."

"Honesty in a world of dishonesty is hard to find. I hope you always bear that in mind."

Seeing an opening I had never really had, I decided to ask a question I'd been thinking about for a long time.

"Professor, sir, may I ask you a question?"

"Of course."

"What does the message actually say? I mean, when you decipher it..."

"I'd like to think we will do that..."

"Yes sir, very good sir."

I was flattered he interrupted to include me. I continued.

"So sir, what do you think the message actually says?"

"Well if it's truly from the Devil I would think it is misleading, yes?"

Well, that didn't answer the question and only made me more confused.

"If it is confusing then why even leave it? Especially if we have to work

so hard to find it only to then…"
"Still not understand?"

"Yes sir, exactly."

"We are in uncharted waters.   The message may, once deciphered, still have little meaning… or be of a philosophical disposition in that it may never be understood."

I stared. That felt so unsatisfying. Even finding the message there might be no real payoff. That took the remaining wind out of my sails and sealed it for me.

In a way, it would make it that much easier to part ways with the crazy old man, and I could focus on what was important.   And I could stop feeling guilty about the fortune he spent to take me overseas with him.

THE SLIPPERY SLOPE

"Mr. Michaels. Take a seat. Please"

My architectural history teacher was probably the most congenial in class, but in person, he was quite stern. I knew why I was here and was dreading it all week. Before I was even settled in he spoke.

"We're here to talk about your grades."

I did my best to sit up. I didn't speak until spoken to. He looked down at the papers in front of him.

"You know exactly what is going on here. If you don't do the work, if you don't show up you are going to fail. If I fail you then you will not graduate. If you do not graduate then you will not have a career."

I nodded. I assumed it was not convincing as it served only to anger him more.

"I'm taking time out of my schedule to remind you of this. This is something you know, Simon. You know what's going to happen."

"Uh, yes, I do. I'm sorry. I don't know…"

"When did you lose your way?"

He looked at me and lowered his voice.

"Is it drugs?"

I tilted my head and think I actually smiled.

"Drugs? Like um…? No. No. No drugs, Mr. Aliota. Never. I mean I have a drink now and then but don't even really like that stuff all that much…"

I was rambling.

"…it's too bitter for the likes of…"

"Simon."

I stopped.

"Yes?"

"Whatever it is, knock it off. You understand? Your mum.."

I stared and he stopped.

"She passed, sir."

The professor stopped as well. He didn't know. I didn't really think about it but I assumed that they all gossiped about their students. Mr. Aliota was too boring for that. He just focused on his teaching and lesson plans. He never got involved with students or gossip or the latest word of mouth.

"Oh, Simon, I am so sorry. Was this recent? I'm sorry…"

"It was a month back."

I shrugged. It was uncomfortable and it made me sad. Now I was both sad and panicked.
I knew my grades had slipped. I hadn't thought they slipped *that* far.

Apparently, they had.

What followed was a mixture of a stern talking-to and a lot of awkward sympathies. He repeatedly explained my lack of focus and slipping grades on my mother's passing. It seemed a bit immoral but I allowed him to think it. The sadness was real so it was easy to play the part.

It was strange that I was less concerned with his condolences and more so with him finding out the true source of my distraction. I felt protective of the reason I had no energy or attention left for this particular class.

In fact, it was then that I wondered if I had any left for my studies at all.

With completely empty promises, and commitments to check in and also "take care of myself" I was on my way.

I took a long walk on the campus and felt the weight of all of it just then. My mum, me squandering my education, my friend setting me up with this. I resented him at that moment. I really didn't like myself either.

There was one person that I despised more than anyone in my frustration and hopelessness. I needed to part ways now and I had one more hurdle.

FOCUS

Today I was to present a summary of the notes I had been working with for the last several months. In fact, it was an entire semester's worth of notes. My mind was spinning from the work and I struggled to remember much about architecture though I know it was in there somewhere.

But not these notes. These were the notes of strange happenings, or completely normal events that the professor had tied together. On top of that were the language translations that I had no business trying to work out. Neither I nor the professor had a degree in language studies.

My frustration was mounting with what I was working with. It was the perfect storm of feeling that I had crossed the line with my studies, that I had read too many notes, and the despair over my mother's death.

"Young man. I will require you to focus on this."

The professor said it in even tones and it was in response to my apparent staring off into the distance thinking about everything but what we were working on.

"On what?! More notes. More notes and nonsense? Things that don't add up?"

I watched his face change as I spoke. I poked at notes on one side of his desk and then ran over to notes taped to the backboard.

"Or there? And… these?! These are not connected as much as you want them to be!"

I was yelling. And waving my arms.

He got up from his desk.

"Now you wait one minute mister."

"Save it. Save it all."

I swept my hands around the room in a grand gesture. I wasn't used to being this mad or frustrated. It was all so absurd.

"I've wasted my… my months! My days! My semesters!"

"Is that what you…?"

No! I've wasted my university education on you and this bullshit. It's all bullshit and you're a crazy old man."

I think I had just screamed it and he looked as if he'd just been called out of the room. He ignored me from that moment on and just gathered some papers as if I was invisible.

He got his hat and made his way out of his office without a word.

I stood there breathing hard and heavily and just stared at the closed door. He hadn't slammed it but he did make sure it was closed firmly.

It was thoroughly unfulfilling for him to leave. I had so much to say and everything had come to a frothy head just then. My mum's death, my slipping grades, my lack of direction this depressing existence of looking for something that didn't exist as a pet project of a man who was obsessed.

Was I a ghost now to him? As far as I was concerned he could fuck right off.

And later that day I learned he did exactly that.

They found him in the courtyard under a tree. It looked like he had gotten a place in the shade and just spread his notes out and just like that had a heart attack and died.

The kids told me later that the old man was so gruff people avoided him for some time even though he was slumped down under the tree in an odd position. They dared not wake him.

They needn't have worried.

He had been dead for hours when they found him. I'll never know if it was my screaming at him that sent him over the edge. He wasn't taking very good care of himself and was missing a lot of sleep by then. His health was suffering like everything else in his life.

But I'll always think it was me that killed him.

Well, not always…

THE PROFESSOR'S FUNERAL 1968

Though things had become tense I discovered that I had genuine feelings of kinship with the professor. Death has a way of clarifying things. I don't know if he was a father figure, or a man of wisdom, or just someone prominent in my formative university years but he meant a lot to me. So at his passing, I was not prepared to see such a lackluster turnout for him.

His funeral consisted simply of the burial at the cemetery with a few words said by a priest. The priest was my age and it made me wonder if any of the other priests just refused. I knew of his falling outs with the faculty and wondered if his extreme views had done the same with the clergy. I couldn't imagine his spouting any of his theories to them.

I was proven right on both accounts.

I cried at his funeral and it was this act that introduced me to a new friend.

"I am so sorry for your loss. You were one of his students?"

It was the young priest. His hair was long and disheveled. I suppose for a while a lot of people looked like one of The Beatles and for some reason, priests always look that way to me.

He shook my hand and I responded.

"Thank you... uh, father...?"

"Tom. Father Tom."

He said it almost to convince himself as much as to introduce himself.

'Oh, hi. I'm Simon. Yes, yes I was a student of his. Well, I was, actually..."

I decided not to try to describe the fact that I wasn't actually a student but was basically a teaching assistant that didn't teach and completely forgot about what I was going to university for in the first place.

It didn't matter what I replied with, I think he was just going through the script they must give priests to help people grieve.

"I appreciate that you came. Not a lot did."

I looked around and there were a few that stood and kept their distance. I never got a chance to even talk to any of them as they scattered right away. Some were older and one was younger but they all looked like they didn't want to be there. I didn't recognize any as current faculty.

I expected it to be raining as all the books and movies always had a big procession of people standing in the rain. I thought when I'd come that I would stay behind and watch from a distance, but the opposite was true; no rain, and I was in the forefront.

Tom was a likable enough fellow, and we chatted a bit more than I expected. He gave me his card and also asked where I was staying and if I had a phone.

I moved into a small flat a while back and the professor's death sort of sealed that idea for me. I associated university with the professor and all of his obsessive ways, so being off campus made me feel normal for a bit, and the money from my mum's estate would be more than adequate to live on for some time.

Besides, it wasn't long before I dropped out anyway. In fact, I unceremoniously did that the next day. I just didn't tell anyone.

Mark Bradford

SHELLEY, 1969

Shelley was the best thing that ever happened to me. She was cool and very into all the social issues of the time. She was the original bra-burning chick of the late sixties and we had a rocky start. It took her a bit to trust that I wasn't after only one thing but once she did we were inseparable. She worked at the local hospital and my teaching job took a lot of our time.

I appreciated the mundanity of just teaching English. Shelley preferred I switch to social studies to make a greater impact, however.

Thanks to a friend of Shelly I met at a protest I was able to land a position at a tertiary university. Oh, you would call it a community college. It's much smaller than university and I dare say their standards are not as high when it comes to whom they hired, and I was grateful for that.

Our relationship was wonderful. We were two young idealistic kids in love. Many a spring and summer were spent admiring and exploring the countryside. Eventually, I was able to get her to stay somewhere with

83

running water and toilets.

We were married one spring in a small ceremony that was comprised mostly of her friends and family. My parents were gone, and I had no living aunts or uncles. My friend Patrick was there.

My mind was on the present and my wife. We flirted with having children and planned for the near future to talk about it again—But we were young and had the rest of our lives to sort it all out. We would probably have children and travel the world.

My life, at last, had a boring enjoyable predictability. The inheritance was partially used up by my frivolous travel, our travels together, and supplementing our income while I got on my feet. We still had a little nest egg for our future and now all we could do was enjoy life.

It seemed, however, that I was not able to escape the professor even after he died for one spring day I received a letter from some attorneys. Or rather, we did, as Shelly had gotten the mail that day and seemed upset.

"What's wrong love?"

My concern was genuine as the majority of her stress was with the establishment and the issues of the day. But she held the letter in her hand. It was already opened even though it was only addressed to me.

"Well, what's this then?"

She slowly handed me the envelope like it was a dead fish. My smile turned into something else as I took it and just pulled out the folded papers—papers that clearly had been refolded and inserted back into the envelope.

I gave her a side glance and found no humor in her eyes. She seemed almost jealous of something, or someone.

I started reading and while doing so I spoke out of the side of my mouth to her with a timid question.

"So you've... already read this then?"

There was no answer.

It was a letter from the attorneys handling the professor's estate. It was the instructions to come to a certain bank to accept a certain key to obtain something that had been left in my care. According to the letter, their ability to reach out to me had been delayed by the professor himself—or rather the instructions in his will. Why he would want them to delay for half a decade made no sense.

"Well, there you have it!"

I looked at her and still felt as if I had done something wrong.

"Shell what is it?"

She looked into my eyes while tears welled up in hers.

"I thought you were leaving Simon. I thought you were leaving me."

I was shocked. I'd never even had the thought in the slightest. It was the happiest point in my life.

"Leaving you? As in a divorce?"

"Yes."

She started crying. There was nothing wrong with our relationship. I was aghast and I just didn't get it. I spent the rest of the day consoling her and assuring her that all was well with us. We even talked about children again.

Though she seemed to be back to normal when I decided to pick up the goods she insisted she come with me. A trip to the attorney's office to sign some paperwork and we were off to the bank.

The bank agent would only allow me into the safe deposit area so Shell reluctantly waited in the teller area. Instead of a little box, this was a larger locker. Inside were three bankers' boxes filled with files—the kids that attorneys love to lug around to show just how much work they've done.

I had to pop back out to get the attendant to come in and carry one of the boxes. They were filled to the top and only made of cardboard. There was just one handwritten note.

"In the event of my untimely death, I wanted to make sure my work survived. It's in your hands now."

He hadn't signed it, nor had he addressed it to me, and that made me wonder if this was just his secret cache whose designated owner would be selected by the attorneys on some unknown criteria.

Shelly's paranoia was rubbing off on me.

She ran to me and grabbed one of the boxes. Apparently, upon receipt, the locker was closed, and I had to sign for acceptance of the boxes. This I did with hesitation.

The old bastard dumped them into my life.

We drove home in silence and the mustiness of the boxes tainted the car's atmosphere. I dared not open a window lest the wind disperse the paperwork to the roadway. The trunk of our underpowered hippie car was just too small.

I also had the impression my wife wanted to keep her eye on them.

When we got home she told me that she wanted to wait til the weekend to go through it with me. Apparently, there was an option. Don't get me wrong, we were very close but this new Shelly had me a little worried. I don't know what she thought was in there.

—

"I talked to Patrick!"

"Patrick? When did he call?"

She made a mock face and thought I was kidding. After some silence, she raised her voice

"At the wedding. Don't be coy with me Simon. I know all about this. I know about all this... secret... *secrets*. I know about the secret project."

I was too confused to be upset.

"What? Paddy told on me at the wedding? And you thought…"

I put my hands on my hips.

"He's such a tea-spiller that man."

My calm reaction just made her more upset.

"Don't! It's not funny. This is not funny!"

"*What's* not funny? What is '*this*'"

She pointed at the box and some of the paperwork I'd carefully removed and placed on my desk.   The desk was so small that two sheets practically covered it. I'd only started sorting through things.

"I know Simon. I know everything."

"Shelly calm down. There's not anything to know. What's to know my dear? You're acting so…"

"This is it, isn't it? This is how I lose you isn't it."

"Lose me?!"

I grabbed her shoulders and brought her to me.

"Shelly you will never lose me."

I smiled when I saw the tiny light in her eyes.

"You'll have to work awfully hard to lose me."

For a second I saw a sadness I didn't recognize and wouldn't understand until much later. But then she brightened. I tried to move her into a different room but we ended up talking for some time surrounded by the boxes and the mess I had made with the papers.   Every so often she would glance at a paper resting here and there. It was an uphill battle that wasn't between me and Shelly but between me and the professor's notes.

Eventually, I won, but it was the start of a rather long conversation about the professor, the notes, and my thoughts on it. Honestly, I hadn't really thought much of the professor's research. My college life was something that I instinctively blocked out. It was a waste of my time and effort and my parents' money. I found I had no real positive feelings toward my time at university.

But in blocking out all the nonsense I had also blocked out my thoughts on 'the secret project' as Shelly called it.

"So what do you think the message says? You never found it?"

She genuinely wanted to know, and the way she asked paradoxically put me on guard, as it was the opposite of the accusatory way she'd been about everything. She'd switched to being fully supportive as if nothing had happened.

"I don't know. That he is everywhere? That if you come looking for him you'll find him? And maybe you shouldn't do that?"

She smiled a terse smile.

"You don't really believe any of this Simon?"

"No of course not. You know how I feel on all of this—Gods and Devils and so forth. This is... archeology of an unusual kind. A language conundrum."

Fortunately, none of the case study notes remained so those never entered the conversation. As far as she knew it was just...notes.

However, I don't think I convinced her. It was all academic, a puzzle, a riddle left with me by an old man who was now gone. In and of itself that was an amazing heirloom. Like a treasure map of sorts. But I had already lost some of my life and opportunity to it and wasn't about to lose any more. I offered to throw it away but she was oddly against it— as if I was hiding something and as long as I was willing to keep the box it meant I was being open.

I spent an exceptional amount of effort making sure my wife was OK, and in turn, I was happy. I felt that I was managing my sanity through managing her happiness and truth be told it was exhausting. After a while, we fell back into our routine and I was mostly convinced that everything was looking up. The only wall I ever hit was joking about moving to the States as a fresh start but due to the argument it caused while she was drinking I never brought it up again.

With her.

"YOU NEVER DID," 1984

Shelley and I lived a stable life, and the box remained on a shelf. Once in a while she would tease me about something being caused by the Devil, and we would have a laugh, but that joke eventually got old.

There was one sunny afternoon I will never forget. I'd just gotten home and was in a sort of fog. There was a stillness in the air like I was holding my breath, lest I disturb it with my exhale.

Shelly's face was unusually intense that day. She smiled, kissed me, and went right to making dinner. I couldn't help but notice the intensity in her eyes.

I did not want to stir things up so paid no mind to it. She wanted no help so I just started rambling on about my work. This went on for some time and it was when she chopped the carrots that she slammed the large knife down onto the cutting board. Her look of exasperation was not hidden by the fact that her eyes were closed. She just stood there with one palm on the counter holding her up and the other tightly gripping the knife.

"Stage Four."

She yelled it, yet said it so quietly.

I stared at the top of her head from across the counter and waited for her to look up. She didn't, so I spoke to her hair and watched her tightly grip the knife.

"Shelly I thought it was only…"

I trailed off. We knew about the cancer but it was early stages. It was manageable. Things were going to be all right. It didn't help that she kept me in the dark. I switched my line of thinking.

"How long have you known? Did you find out today? When was your last…"

"Stop it!"

She looked up. She was angry. Her eyes were distant.

"What? What have I…"

"Stop it with your positive attitude, Simon."

She said my name as if imploring me. I was so confused.

"I just want to make dinner. Can't we be real? *Can* we be real? From now on?"

"Sweetheart of course we can why wouldn't…"

I spoke quickly to make amends — to make everything OK again.

"You have no control over this Simon. None."

That was when she let go of the knife and started crying. In a creaky, weak, defeated voice she said three words to me that I'll never forget.

"You never did."

—

We tried to make the most of the time left for us, but that was made difficult by her reserve. I spent the rest of the nest egg on helping with treatments and exploring different options for her.

Her brother Sam had an on-again-off-again relationship with her. I know you normally use that term to describe a romantic relationship, but it seemed like sometimes they were family and sometimes they weren't. It was mostly just apathy between the two of them with short bouts of one of them caring.

Now he was family, and it seemed that this would be how things would be until she got better. At least part of me hoped. He could piss off once she was better because he really didn't add to her life, and I think the stress of their sometimes-estranged relationship added to her pain.

Imagine my surprise when Sam told me in no uncertain terms that he felt the same about me.

He shook my hand and as always gripped it tighter than was required. His smile was not genuine.

"Hello, Simon."

He'd never ask how she was—just greet me then go see her. She was laying down so I was a formality in the way. I tried to be cordial and wondered if he could see that I'd recently been crying.

He walked to our room and closed the door. Lately, I wasn't invited to the chats and I no longer cared. He could say what he wanted as long as he was supportive.

This time I heard his voice rise a bit just before the door was opened. He emerged and wouldn't look at me and walked towards his coat. It hadn't even had time to dry from the rain.

"Sam. What's…"

He flung his raincoat on and water flew in a pattern around him like the feathers on a peacock.

His eyes were steel and his cosmetically-corrected teeth formed a perfect smile.

"Well that does it, doesn't it, Simon?"

"I, ah…"

He stood at his full height.

"You. How much more of this do you think she could have taken? You're to blame, man."

It was my turn to be angry.

"What the hell are you talking about?"

He swung at me and had it not been for the raincoat getting in the way I wouldn't have been able to dodge. I yelled as quietly as I could.

"Are you fucking mental?!"

He put up his hands as if to box and with his fists between us started to accuse.

"You! You bastard. This is your fault. You stressed her. How can she heal with you being gone and bangin' on about your nonsense? What the holy fuck."

"Now wait a minute Sammy how dare…"

He swung and this time connected. It hurt but I didn't go down and tried to return the favor. We landed some blows and I remember us both screaming quietly as some part of us still remembered a loved one was slowly dying nearby.

We both made the same points and the same case about the other being the one adding stress and killing her. Our jabs were not just physical and I think those hurt more. I don't know how long we fought but we were exhausted when we finally heard her.

That day she died. She called to us—no doubt hearing the fight and wanting to stop it. To this day I'll never know what she said and all I can think is that she was saying one of our names. No matter what I come up with, my memory will always blame me. See, if she was calling for him it meant she wanted him to be the person who comforts her as she passed. If she was calling to me it was to stop fighting.

The mind is a terrible thing.

THE EX-PRIEST, 1990

Father Tom was with us until the last moment. Outside of the professor, I had not really connected with anyone else save for my wife. With both of their passing, Tom became the closest thing to a friend I had. Eventually, one day while having beers I shared more than I should have and did the one thing I vowed never to do—I had a debate on religion with a priest.

As it turned out it was not as bad as I expected. The more I shared the more he nodded.

I made the usual points that I'm sure people make to priests all the time. I told of my personal experiences as well as what I'd seen. None of it made any sense. I went on and on and on. It was mostly an intoxicated rant and soon it turned from a debate into just me complaining about my circumstances.

Was I enlightening him, or was he just being compassionate as after all my partner had just passed away?

"Uh-huh."

He nodded again.

"Yes Tom you said that before. In fact you said that about fifty times."

It came out a bit snarky.

"Simon, what do you want me to say?"

"Want? I want a good listener but compassion is not enough."

"I know that well."

I put my glass down harder than I thought, but fortunately, no beer was lost in the process.

"Oh, I'm sure you do."

I was not being kind. I wanted a reaction. I wanted more. I wanted... I wanted what the professor wanted.

Honesty.

"I miss him."

He was confused.

"Him?"

"Yes, the professor. I miss him. With him, I could be honest."

I sipped from my glass, closed my eyes, and drowned in both beer and sorrow.

"That's all I want you to know."

I spoke it into the glass without looking.

"That's what we all want Simon, but sometimes that's hard, and..."

"Ha!"

I slammed the glass down again. I had enough.

"Oh come on. You're the last person who should say that. I mean *really*."

I rolled my eyes at him and regret how mean I'd become. He didn't speak and gave me more rope with which to hang myself.

"You of all people Tom. Your empire is built on lies, ignoring the obvious. Of having…"

"Faith?"

I guffawed. "It's not all about faith you know. You can't play that damn card with me. Especially now. She's gone, he's gone. Nothing happens now. Now I'm alone.

"You have me."

I stared at him and felt a tear running down my cheek. It might have been the beer from the glass rim. I don't know. I was drunk.

"Tom, why do you even do this?"

"Do what? I'm just trying to…"

"You want to comfort me until oblivion. You want to make me feel better until I simply don't exist."

"And?"

"What?! That's not comforting."

"That's what you said you want."

"What?"

"Honesty."

I tilted my head and tried to keep my thoughts at least partially clear I as filled with emotion. I looked like a dog hearing a distant siren.

"Tom you're gonna have to explain... I don't know if you know this but I'm drunk. I'm drinking here see?"

I tilted my glass demonstrably. The beer sloshed.

"Simon. What difference does it make if there is an afterlife or not when you are grieving?"

"Uh, because if there is one then I can believe the fairy tale that they are all right."

"But you will still miss them."

"Yes but... maybe not as much?"

"No, that's not how that works. Your grief is not based on thinking on whether they are in a better place, it is based on their absence in your life."

Philosophy.

"Tom not now. I just want to be sad. I want to be fuckin' sad, ya feel me?"

He turned his body on the stool to once again face the bar. He didn't speak for a while.

I could feel my breathing while I thought. Finally, he interrupted the silence I'd created.

"I think I'm done."

I turned to him, slightly alarmed that he was standing, had paid his tab, and was leaving the bar. I opened my eyes wide. He was not. He was still sitting there with me.

"What do you mean?"

With this. He pointed to his collar. I was alarmed. It was a really bad joke and a ploy to gain my confidence. I just squinted my disbelief at him.

He looked over his shoulder as if we were being followed by a Cardinal or two.

"I mean I am done. I'm leaving. No no not the bar." He took a sip of his drink as if that would somehow affirm his point.

"Well why?" I was confused.

"Because I've seen too much suffering."

I was still skeptical. This came out of nowhere. Was I the last straw?

"Well why though, Tom? I guess I am confused. I don't know how this works. I don't have experience with…religious studies."

Neither one of us believed what I'd just said. It was an intended pun, compliments of the alcohol. He almost smiled. I just wanted to keep drinking and get back to my sorrows. I didn't have any brain cells for this.

"It's easier than you think. Sort of like dropping out of University."

"Is this a priest trick? I focus on your absurdities and then I forget my problems? Focus outward so I don't have to focus inward? Good Samar…"

I stopped. He looked sincerely sad and lost.

We spent the next hour talking about the why of it. He ran through the suffering, the death, the sadness.

Oddly with every story he told I rebuked it with the positives of his work.

With every pain, I offered compassion. With each mention of suffering, I mentioned his presence. With each burden, I mentioned his willingness to carry some of it. He had indeed tricked me into being the advocate of positivity. Bravo.

Finally, with some intoxicated frustration, he got loud.

"Don't you see?! It's pointless. All of it. I can't end the suffering. It doesn't make any sense. I do God's work, time and time again, but it's affecting me. There's no real mental help for people in my position."

"But what about before? The compassion, the part about grief?"

"I made it up. It doesn't really matter. Whatever I can say to make you feel better, Simon. That's what it's all about right? But it feels... What did you say? You wanted honesty? It feels...*dishonest.*"

I was numb. There is nothing that will make you feel more empty than discovering that the person comforting you was lying the whole time.

But I wasn't going to believe it.

"Tom there's gotta be more."

I waived the bartender over for refills. The seriousness was detracting from my inebriation and that just wouldn't do. I stared. He stared. He looked away. What seemed like minutes passed as we waited for the refills and the bartender to give us some distance.

"I had an affair."

"When?"

"I had two."

"What?!"

"Why are you so surprised Simon? You've said yourself that it's unnatural to prevent intimate contact like that. That it just leads to..."

I nodded. He continued while shaking his head.

"It sure does."

"Twice."

"It's common. People are weak, vulnerable."

"I…" I had trouble finding words.

"That includes me!"

"OK, ok, Tom. I get it. You have ample reason to leave. But is it a case of just being asked to leave but publicly 'resigning?'"

I was glad he was honest. I was back in that particular comfort zone at least.

"I met someone."

"Tom!"

I smiled. I was actually happy for him, but all this information was coming out of nowhere in a rush. I'm sure the beer probably helped.

"She's great. I couldn't hide it anymore."

I put my hand on his shoulder as if he'd just told me he was engaged.

"Tom that's great! I'm relieved. So it's not the other stuff you told me. I…"

"Simon we are sort of having two conversations here."

My head hurt. I told my brain cells to do me one last favor of clarity and made a simple request.

"Tom, sort it all for me and I'll shut up. Please."

"OK. It was all the suffering that I was navigating that led me to the two affairs. I'm calling them affairs because they were with married women. The women were grieving. Do you know how easy that is? That's all they want. I didn't take advantage of them!"

He looked around and lowered his voice.

"I didn't. I didn't have to. That's all they wanted was comfort, and for someone to love them. They needed those moments. The second one was when it hit me—all that suffering and I'm powerless. Anything I could do to make them feel better was just misleading them. So that happened. They found out about the second one but were happy to sweep it under the rug. That's when my opinion changed."

I waited to make sure he was finished. He took a sip of his beer so I inquired.

"And your girlfriend? When did that happen?"

"A few months after the last affair. She knows about them. Her problem was that they were married, not that I sought intimacy as a priest, or that I tried to bring them solace."

"So you are leaving the priesthood, and have a girlfriend. Well, all things considered that is positive—it's where you want to be."

I had one last question.

"And your faith?"

"Yes, what of it."

"Oh, I thought you said you were done—that it was just all suffering and so forth."

"Well yes."

He hadn't made the same conclusion. People are complex.

"So you still have faith."

"Simon. Yes, of course."

He put his hand on my shoulder.

"Yes, it has not affected my faith. That's not how faith works."

He smiled a convincing smile. I felt alone. Why couldn't I find this faith? He'd been through the wringer. He'd seen as much suffering as me and felt the futility of helping. He knew the system he was in was flawed.

But he still believed. I envied that comfort.

After that discussion I didn't see Tom much—he was busy nurturing his relationship with the new girl, and since I had no one I would just be a third wheel. It would be a long time before we could do couples' dates, if ever.

CAFE: 2:30 PM

"Mark you look uncomfortable."

I blinked self-consciously and I think I sat up a little, and then I lied.

"Uncomfortable? Well no—not at all…"

"Yes you are."

He winked at me. That didn't help. The story and all this talk of religion were making me feel uncomfortable.

"Does discussing faith make you feel uncomfortable Mark?"

"Well, no, discussing it doesn't."

I smiled. I boasted.

"I assume by now you see I have pretty good stamina for talking, Simon."

"But not religion." He countered quickly.

"Um, I actually taught Sunday school for a little while."

"Oh? How was that?"

"Well, we made a lot of projects with glue and noodles."

He smiled. I was searching for something devious. I couldn't find it. My inability to find his motivation was disturbing. Maybe that was what made me feel uncomfortable; maybe it was that he told the story with an absolutely straight face and that he truly believed what he was telling me.

"Simon, I'm not a big fan of people defining or rewriting my reality. I don't think anyone is."

He sipped what was probably his fourth cup of tea with a twinkle in his eye.

"Mark if you feel that way in a simple chat with an old man, imagine how all of this felt for me for the last five decades."

I stuck out my bottom lip in a sort of frown and just said "Hmm." He had a point but I thought at any minute this would turn into the *And so this is why you should repent* or *So here's a pamphlet* and *This is why you are a bad person but I can help.*

I was staring and thinking and not talking. We had an awkward few seconds of silence. Well, it was awkward for me.

"It doesn't feel good, does it?"

This was almost too much.

"Simon, I don't have to believe anything you're saying. I'm enjoying this chat with you. Is it important that I believe it?"

"Why do you think I am telling you?"

I laughed and it surprised me. I had become tense and defensive and I welcomed the guffaw that just came from me.

"I don't know. Because you want to share? Because you enjoy being a storyteller? Because you're retired?" *Because you're an old lonely man.*

He leaned forward the tiniest bit and looked into my eyes and spoke. It was rather intense. It's one thing to sit across from someone and listen passively and another thing entirely to feel they've invaded your space, stare into your eyes, and speak directly to you as if they're revealing some universal secret or conspiracy.

"*Because I promised I would not.*"

My disrespectful eye roll was completely lost on him.

I excused myself and used the restroom. The manager gave me an odd look and looked at his watch as if to tell me that I had been there all day. I had been. It felt odd to leave him with that cliffhanger but honestly, I was a little overwhelmed.   I've been invited to two secret societies and I've turned them down. They were…disappointing and all of my friends know which ones they were. And most of my friends think I was dumb to turn them down. But nothing is ever as cool as you think it's going to be. Or maybe that's me.

And this was one of those cases. I stared at the wall in silence thinking about his story and how I thoroughly rejected it. It wasn't just a simple story, this was a rather long life story being told to me and I just wanted the punch line. But was that really the problem? Was it that my writing was on hold because all I could think about was this story?   My mind kept trying to find weak points and inconsistencies. I wanted to be able to say *Aha, people don't react like that. You made that up!* I couldn't even find his ulterior motive.

Until now.

Now I left him telling me that last line. 'That he promised *not* to.' What did that mean?   I was fairly sure I would return to the table and my laptop would be gone. And so would he. Did he tell me a half-day-long story so that I'd eventually trust him, go to the bathroom, and then he could steal it?
A cough.

The man behind me was clearing his throat and wanted to use the urinal.

I think I had been staring off for some time.

I finished and made sure not to take ten minutes to wash my hands as the poor guy behind me had waited long enough.

I returned to the table. My laptop was still there, so was the giant stack of musty papers and the old man.

He smiled but looked concerned.

I wasn't the only one that thought the other would just abruptly leave.

"I can stop, Mark."

He looked genuinely concerned for my well-being. There was kindness and concern in his eyes.

"Simon, no, of course not. Please continue. We should probably grab a bite."

It was times like this that I wondered why I always pushed myself outside my comfort zone—especially with people. I always got burned. I *did* feel uncomfortable, but I thought his story would be over soon, and it was nice to be a good listener.

He immediately got up and ordered us some mediocre cafe food and continued his story.

At that point, I figured he probably had no one else to share with, and that he'd found a cafe friend. There were worse ways to spend a Sunday, and doing something like this seemed to be in character for me. I would listen and absorb and laugh about it later over a beer with a friend.

Mark Bradford

MOVING TO THE U.S.

When I thought there was really nothing left for me I decided to make the trek here, to the U.S. I had never been, and even when we went on holiday we never crossed the pond. But there was an emptiness that I thought I could fill by coming here.

It was easier than I thought to once again get a job in education. I think it's the accent—people in the U.S. think you're smarter when they hear it.

I was OK with using that to my advantage.

There were some hard times and I bounced around for some time before I found a city to my liking. And for a rather long time, it was just work, eat and sleep. I never really met a replacement for Shelley. Though I left her back in that cemetery thousands of miles away I thought about her often.

I made some friends and drank some beer and eventually liked the taste and temperature of it here. But those were empty years.

Oddly the thing that filled my world was the thing that seemed to have once emptied it.

I was sitting in my little apartment and had a knock at the door. It was my neighbor from down the hall—a nice younger man but I never really connected as he liked to talk and talk. When I opened the door he immediately started talking loudly and standing too close.

"Hey Simon! How's it going? Hey so the landlord just called—I was talking to him anyway about the light again you know—oh I probably didn't tell you that but anyway, he called. He wanted me to let everyone I know that there's water in the basement and that if we have anything that isn't stored in plastic containers—you know we are supposed to do that—his rules, not mine."

He laughed nervously.

"So yeah you should go down there—I'm gonna go down there now and just check but I'm very good about my containers."

He exhausted me.

"Thanks, Scott. You go ahead without me. I'll be along later. I'm in the middle of something right now."

"Are you sure? I mean I can wait—if you want—like not forever of course... haha!"

I smiled and then just slowly closed the door. He was the type to stay in the conversation as long as you'd let him. When I thought enough time and passed I did indeed go downstairs to the storage area. There was only a bit of water and I did have everything in the proper plastic bins. But up on a higher shelf was a cardboard banker's box—the professor's notes. Shelley and I had consolidated all the notes into one box years ago—a task that took over a week and had me walking on eggshells for some time afterward.

It seemed vulnerable just sitting up there and I imagined it falling to the cement floor and wicking up all the water. I just had the strong urge to move it, so I took it back to my apartment for safer keeping.

That was when I smelled it for the first time in over ten years. That mustiness, the smell of the papers and folders that you can't buy here in the States, and I think it probably had a hint of the professor's cologne.

I put them in the closet of my tiny apartment so there was no place I could escape the weak but ever-present scent—even when I slept.

At least that was my reasoning for all the dreams. Time and time again I would dream about the professor, and my mum, and times gone by—and the notes were always there. It wasn't long before I had a rather bad day at work and came home to drown my sorrow in beer.

I was sitting on my floor in my underwear and decided to just grab the box and dump it onto the floor.

I sat there with my legs spread around the pile and now the scent was overwhelming. I spent that night reading through the notes again and bringing myself up to speed. Everything I had blocked was now returning. Every moment I'd experienced was brought back in vivid detail. They say smell is powerful like that. It was something else.

From that moment on I was back in my college years working feverishly for the professor. I started going to libraries again, reading things online, and looking up research papers. So much knowledge at my fingertips! I even started watching the news for confirmations.

I found a lot of them.

Everything made sense now.

TO FIND IS TO REVEAL

"This is the best I can do. Because…"

She was frustrated. She was the best linguist I could afford. I hired her and we met at the local library. She was able to pre-select books to be sent to it. It took some time for them to get there but she had been using them for about a week. It made sense to me to have as many resources locally with someone I could…talk to. This telephone nonsense just wasn't working for me and we didn't have all the technology you have today. I wasn't going to have a video call any time soon, and we were talking about a lot of images, so I need to show my notes and work to my assistant.

Assistant.

Not since the professor did I use that word and it brought back surprisingly happy memories.

But she was fumbling. Her translation wasn't going smoothly and she was confused. The frustration was making her cranky so I had to manage her feelings along with her results.

She showed me what she had come up with and it didn't make sense. Or rather, it made too much sense. I felt she had just projected her expectations on top of the translation. This was something the professor painstakingly avoided, and part of that pain was let out on me.

Obviously, you have to have some sort of expectation and when things come together you see the pattern and even the intent. But this almost seemed like a note from her to me. It was in a rather informal language. And the words made no sense because...

Then it hit me as the words came together. The words were referencing things not yet created, things not yet imagined.

Without giving you a crash course in linguistics, the only way I can explain it is this—imagine that you have to tell someone in ancient Egyptian to remember to start the coffeemaker tomorrow and that you prefer the hazelnut-vanilla coffee. They have no reference for what a coffeemaker is, no understanding of electricity. And if you need them to travel to your house to do it your address would make no sense— especially if the street name had no comparable word.

But that's exactly what it was. It was a street name, the name of a business, and a time. There was no date.

I looked at my watch. I could only assume it was today.

"What is it, Mr. Michaels?"

"What? Oh. It's what I was looking for I think."

She seemed to think I was lying to pacify her as if I didn't want to tell her she failed.

"*What you're looking for?* The words don't make any sense. I've never seen them used that way. It's as if they were poorly translated. Almost like..."

"Like someone tried to translate English into this obscure language?"

"Yes."

"Like the way a child would try to use a limited vocabulary to relay something complex."
"Well, I don't know about that. Maybe it's a dialect or a usage that we've never uncovered. I think that's a number, but it's not supposed to be next to that symbol."

Her eyes widened as she appreciated the opportunity. I believe that part of the reason she took the job with me was that she thought I'd stumbled on something overlooked by others, and being able to attach her name to these findings was worth far more than the pittance I was able to muster for her. I had to calm her enthusiasm.

"No, no I don't think we discovered a unique dialect of caste usage, I think we just found something interesting."

I looked at my watch again.

"Well now what then?"

I could see she was exhausted.

"Well, now I better not be late."

I thanked her and stumbled out—almost knocking over the pile of books. I'm sure she thought I was crazy and probably resented me for how I'd treated her through the whole process.

I didn't even have to get a cab and instead just ran. The autumn breeze was nice and the cold on my face woke me up as I made my way there. It was literally just a few blocks away.

This etching in this obscure language, which seemed out of place over a thousand years ago, combined words that had no business being together, and spelled out a note. It was obvious.

It was a note to *me*, to tell me to meet *him*, at a local cafe, at three o'clock.

Today.

—

It took me only minutes and a glance at my watch again revealed that it was 2:55 pm. I wouldn't be late.

Walking in I smelled the various brews of coffee and tea. It was pleasant enough and I scanned the customers. My heart was beating fast and I knew it was only in part due to the running I'd done.

Then I realized that I had no idea what he would look like. I kept looking and must have appeared as if I was on a first date nervously looking for the woman.

I looked around and the place was full. Every booth was filled with at least two people. I was the only person that wasn't a pair or a group.

Fortunately, the counter was far from the door so no one was asking me what I wanted, as a drink was the farthest from my mind. I kept looking and looking and then my heart sank.

Standing out like a sore thumb was the only unoccupied booth. It was empty and the sight of it made me feel completely out of place. I looked at my watch. It was 2:59 pm. Yes, 2:59 pm on a random Tuesday and I had run to the nearest cafe because of what I thought was in a thousand-year-old note written to me before this area was even populated, the buildings were built, and I was yet to be born in an entirely different country. I think I was at my lowest point then. I took a deep breath and desperately wanted sanity to seep in. Perhaps this would be the start of my way back from the madness, and it would start with a cup of proper tea.

3:00 pm. Seeing that on my watch made me smile as it solidified how silly I'd become, and my thoughts went to the nice girl that I had mistreated. Yes, I'd have the tea, take a breath and apologize to her. Whatever little money I had left I'd use to pay her. She worked so hard to search for the thing that didn't exist. I would sit at the booth, alone, and just stare. Yes. This would be the therapy I needed. I could actually feel the muscles in my neck relaxing.

I looked up to make sure newcomers hadn't taken the only empty booth.

It was too late though.   It was now occupied by a man, and he immediately raised his cup to me.

It was him.

TO REVEAL IS TO SUMMON

"Go ahead."

I had already made my way to the booth and sat down. He watched me the entire way and with every step I could feel who he really was. I felt colder the closer I came. Each step made it more real as the rest of the cafe blurred out of existence.

He had already ordered for me. A cup of what I assumed was tea showed me how hot it was with the steam that wafted from it.

The man sat across from me and stirred his coffee. He was relatively handsome, taller, and had black hair. I didn't see any horns and he was clean-shaven. He wore a suit jacket but no tie. All in all, he was pleasant to look at. He told me to speak so I spoke.

"I guess my first question is why?"

"It always is."

"Always? You mean there have been others. We were not the first?"

I was already shocked. He hadn't yet answered my question and yet I was already feeling confused. He smiled and continued.
"You think that you and the professor were the first to discover all this and put it together?"

Surprisingly I remembered my initial question.

"That wasn't my question. My question was why you did this."

"Well, why do *you* think I did this?"

He was elusive and our back and forth was anything but simple. I watched him sip his coffee and I tried to continue.

"You are not answering my question. I thought—well—my expectation was that you would chat with me and answer all of my questions."

"Is that what you thought?"

"Yes."

He stared at me as if I was a dog learning a new trick. I couldn't wait any longer so I just blurted out what I thought.

"I think you did this because you are bored. Or you need recognition. Or some sort of worship from people. Maybe it keeps you going, or it gives you your power? Maybe you just get a perverse pleasure from watching people suffer and you had to tell everyone...someone? Or maybe there are rules in place that force you to play this game."

He seemed satisfied that he'd made me give in and answer for him. He looked around the cafe, smiling and sometimes returning the smile of a cafe-goer. He hid in plain sight and looked like he was enjoying his coffee. Finally, he sat back a tiny bit and gave me his answer.

"Simon. What if there are no rules? What if I am the supreme being in your reality?"
"But the professor always said that your biggest trick was convincing

everyone you didn't exist."

"Yes. It is a popular quote. Your professor did not coin it."

"Oh? Who did?"

"Well, me of course—through various individuals. I planted the seed."

Again he was misleading and going off on tangents.

"But that doesn't seem important. Why would you want to convince people you didn't exist only to leave this elaborate trail? This message that spans through the ages, and all religions?"

"Exactly."

"Well, what?"

I was so confused.

"Simon, that is not my biggest trick. You are correct. What did you learn from all these years with the professor? From the actual message itself?"

"That you are in the details. That you are in everything?"

"Right. I am in everything."

He tapped his coffee cup with his fingernail, looked around the cafe, and then surveyed the sky through the window. He looked back into my eyes and continued. It wasn't a man in a booth sweeping his head around to have a glance, he was surveying everything—from the matter that made the coffee cup to the building and all the humans there to the sky and beyond. It was a grand gesture. I felt the weight of it.

"So then, what is my biggest trick? What have I convinced people of that is not true?"

"Well if you *do* exist, and you are not trying to convince them that you do *not*… then it is…"
"Yes?"

"Oh my God…"

He nodded, graciously, and looked pleased as if he'd just then introduced himself. He did. Or rather, *I* just did.

I just stared at him.   I was frozen in place—not just in body, but in mind… and more.

I couldn't say it, but he knew I knew. He looked so satisfied. He smiled a smile that was completely devoid of any comfort, compassion, and humanity. And he spoke words that echoed in not only my ears but my soul.   I remember this more vividly than anything I have ever experienced, and I know nothing will ever compare to that moment. No triumph, no loss, no shock, no moment of realization—nothing. Frozen in place and in time, helpless, I stared back and watched him answer.

"My biggest trick was not convincing people that I did not exist, it was convincing them that God *did*."

The man—the creature, the being—that sat across from me sipping the same coffee as me, out of the same kind of mug I was drinking out of, was infinitely powerful, infinitely knowing, and was in fact the sole supreme being in my reality. The game he chose to play was to convince others that he was the lesser of two beings—that another being was more powerful and was the essence of love, and kindness.   And because of this, throughout the ages he would play the bad guy, all the while doing anything he wanted to his subjects.

He was free to torment them, to make them suffer, to play with them, to treat them as pets and playthings. He could kill puppies and children. He could cause the most horrific of happenings, and more importantly choose not to intervene. He had the power and the knowledge—just like God is supposed to have. But we give God a pass. When we don't understand we say 'He moves in mysterious ways.' When people suffer we blame the Devil, or we say there is a greater plan. When someone is hurting we give them hope instead of help.

If he announced himself as a supreme being that delighted in the torments and suffering of his creations they would cease to suffer. They would quickly expire with no reason to live. They would revolt and keep to themselves.

If he proclaimed he was an omnipotent and omniscient god then we would expect him to intervene and to make everything good, just, and whole.

But if he created a god for us to worship, and behind the scenes was actually in control, then he is free to play his game. He could blame all the bad things on himself or the shortcomings of man. Instead of revolting, people would just rally against what they thought he was — the enemy of light and kindness. They would worship the god they thought they were worshipping, all the while actually worshipping *him* — the cause of their pain, the entity that did not help.

He had answered all the questions I could not answer, which was what caused me to be an atheist in the first place. None of it made sense.

It did now. In one horrible sentence.

There was no God. There was just The Devil, and he *was* God.

I sat there and absorbed what my brain had just unwound in front of me. It was too much; it was more than too much — it was literally *everything*. The entirety of life was there in front of me, and it smelled of sulfur. I feel like I must have stared through him for some time. I felt nothing but the numbness of realization. I don't even know if I was breathing.

But eventually, I took a deep breath and my eyes refocused on the being before me.

He still hadn't answered the why of it. I looked down at my tea for an eternity and looked back at him when I finally found the energy to ask in a creaky, timid voice.

"But... *why* though?"

"Why do I do what I do? Or why did I take a particular interest in you, Simon Michaels?"

That made me freeze again. The way he looked into my eyes, the way I was getting personal attention from him, the way he said my name... I felt singled out as if I was his only subject in Hell.

I repeated what he'd said—quietly. He took it as a question.

"Particular interest…?"

"I take particular interest in anyone who finds the message. Is it not delightful to experience the meaning yourself? Is it not enlightening to actually embrace what the message is trying to tell you? Do you not think that it helped you by causing you to experience a more intense version than the average person experiences?'

I stared and realized that there *had* been hope in me, because at that point what little there was left forever.

"You wanted to know. None of it made sense but now you understand how it works."

He raised his mug to me. I had one last question.

"But now what? What do I do with this information?"

I knew that he would just stare at me and wait for me to offer an answer to my own question. But before I could answer, he said his last words to me:

"The Devil's in the details."

Mark Bradford

CAFE 4:20 PM - TO SUMMON IS TO DIE

I couldn't hide the shock on my face. More than once people had walked by and overheard a word or two. I did everything I could to make it look like we were discussing a movie instead of the man's life story.

I simultaneously had a look of shock, a smile, and probably a bit of panic.

Simon's eyes were tear-filled as if he'd just climbed a great flight of stairs and was relieved. He had a distant smile now and seemed to look through me.

I'd spent the entire day listening to Simon talk. I was mesmerized and we'd shared two meals together along with countless cups of coffee and tea.

I looked at the old man before me and tried to decipher the look on his face. Had he just told me the most elaborate story I'd ever heard? Was this something he did periodically? Was I so naive as to not know this was some sort of well-known movie from the '30s or some tall tale? I'd never heard of such a thing—ever. It was a deceptively simple concept that could be encapsulated in one sentence. That kind of conciseness was like gold to me, and something that authors strive to find. And yet it made a compelling story. I wanted to ask others at the cafe if they'd ever heard him tell this story to anyone else.

I had so many questions. If they weren't the first then who else had found the message? Who were the others that had an audience with the devil? Did they write it down? What did he mean when I left for the bathroom? He didn't mention the promise. Was it to the devil? Finally, I spoke.

"Simon… It's an amazing story."

I sat back a bit in my chair. He looked so intense now as if he'd just run a marathon. His eyes were wide as if he was on a drug far stronger than caffeine. Not for the first time I questioned why I was talking to him. Why did I always welcome random strangers like this only to be burned by some bizarre action or story that made me feel like I wanted to run away? I could tell he wanted a better reaction from me. He wanted me to have the same epiphany—to stand up and shout. He wanted what he just told me to have an effect on me beyond what was apparent. He just stared at me as if he was a magician that had just performed the greatest trick and was in disbelief because the audience was silent.

He took a deep breath and then spoke loudly, imploringly, and with exasperation. He ticked off all the points in his story that I was supposed to connect, it seemed.

"Young atheist gets promising job at prestigious college, and then gets embroiled in religious pursuits and forsakes his career. Professor commits his lifetime to decipher a message only to die alone in obscurity and be thought mad. Man finds true love only to have her taken away from him as he slowly watches her suffer. Man watches as his priest friend finds the love missing from his life. Young man takes up the mantel of mad professor and then actually meets the Devil. He is given knowledge that few have ever been given—life-altering and reality-shattering only to be told he can never tell any…"

That was when he shoved his pile across the table and grabbed his chest.

I bolted upright as his other arm lashed out on the table, spilling his tea—straight for his precious pile of old papers.

I'm embarrassed to say that I grabbed them and in that second was more concerned with him losing his life's work than helping him. But I wasn't the only person who'd seen and heard his collapse. A woman ran over to assist him as I shook my head to tell her I had no idea what was happening. My eyes implored her to do whatever she could to help him. She was helping with his arm, and his chest and the other women from her table were running over and surrounding him. It propelled me backward like a buoy in a sea of nurses.

I was by the stairs now and watching from afar. It seemed like there was so much yelling that there was no sound and before I knew it paramedics were there as if they'd been parked outside the whole time. More and more people were crowding the space and a rush of people were leaving to make room so I had no choice but to descend the stairs, lest I'd either fall or get shoved into the garbage can at the top of the landing.

It seemed to make the most sense to wait outside. I looked for the ambulance that had produced the timely paramedics.

I backed out through the entrance and scanned the street and those on the outside patio. Everything was calm and normal, and sunny.

Just when I thought it was all a dream two of the paramedics ran out and disappeared toward the parking lot. In seconds they came back with a cart. He was in good hands now.

I walked briskly to my car and put my laptop and the stack of papers in my trunk. My trunk would probably smell musty for some time after that, I mused. I felt guilty as if I was stealing from someone, but I'd find out his name and see him in the hospital.

That was my big mistake. I never should have left his side.

I had so many more questions—not the least of which was 'Why me?' Why did he decide to visit me one day and then spend the entire day telling me this story—a story that apparently came with decades of documentation that was now conveniently in my trunk?

What was I supposed to do now? Was I under the same rule he apparently was? He hadn't made me make any promises, nor had I received this directly from the Devil.

I would love to tell you that the paperwork was returned to its rightful owner. I would like to tell you that Simon Michaels did not die moments after leaving the cafe.

But I cannot. It's a bit more complicated than that. My trunk was not musty it turns out. The paperwork never found its owner because I was unable to locate either ever again. Now that you've read the book will I suffer the same fate? I assume not since I did not seek this out, as far as I know. And in turn, you also will not suffer the same fate.

If you want more I will just risk giving you the same phrase that I was given.

"The Devil's in the details."

Mark Bradford

EPILOGUE

Sometimes I think I write epilogues for myself and not the audience. Writing a novel is an experience that requires one to come up for air at the end—and like a very long roller coaster ride forces one to say "Wow, that was something, huh."

There needs to be a discussion, an unwinding, and a commiseration.

So if you'll commiserate with me I would like to talk about the ride.

I have always been adamant about first-person stories. I find them—rather smugly—to be the respite of new authors and those that focus mostly on the spicy urban fantasy genre.

In addition, a first-person story drastically narrows the options of the author as you can only talk about and describe what the narrator (the actual person talking about his experiences) was able to experience.

As someone who wrote a trilogy in the voice of an omnipotent third-person with a number of simultaneous things happening and tracked, this kind of method is a jarring and restrictive endeavor. But since this was a retelling of a lifelong journey from the perspective of the old man who told it to me there was no other way to tell it properly.

I hope you enjoyed the first-person tale.

ABOUT THE AUTHOR

Mark frequents cafes and often experiences mediocre coffee. He lives near water and a beautiful green landscape that is covered in snow more often than not. Sometimes the people are crabby, sometimes they are friendly.

Follow Mark on Instagram for announcements and things related to his content—books, podcasts, etc.

`@authormarkbradford`

Have a book club? You can usually find book club questions for his books on his website for all endeavors:

`markbradford.org`

<u>Books by Mark Bradford</u>

The Status Game
The original book on status and online dating.

The Status Game II
How status is the key to all relationships - business and personal.

OneSelf
Faith of a simpler, more direct kind. Or just nonsense?

Alchemy for Life: Formulas for Success
Everything you need to know about Life Coaching in one book. And 16 formulas for success.

Three Voices
The three voices we use to communicate with ourselves and others. An experimental psychology book endorsed by a clinical psychologist. It literally can help you with the voices in your head.

The Sword and the Sunflower trilogy:
The Sword and the Sunflower
1,000 years in the future a grieving father takes on his last job to kill a man for untold wealth but what he finds instead changes him and the world forever.

Amira
The sequel and epic conclusion to The Sword and the Sunflower

Upside Down
The 1,000-year history of The Saints.

<u>Coming soon:</u>

The Status Game III: Discover Your Gages
The three-book compendium with workbook.

If you liked this book
I would appreciate it if you took a minute
to review it.

You aren't obligated to do that of course.

www.ingramcontent.com/pod-product-compliance
Lightning Source LLC
Chambersburg PA
CBHW071920220626

47052CB00002B/428